A Note to Parents and Caregivers:

With a focus on math, science, and social studies, *Read-it!* Readers support both the learning of content information and the extension of more complex reading skills. They encourage the development of problem-solving skills that help children expand their thinking.

 The PURPLE LEVEL presents basic topics and objects using high frequency words and simple language patterns.

 The RED LEVEL presents familiar topics using common words and repeating sentence patterns.

 The BLUE LEVEL presents new ideas using a larger vocabulary and varied sentence structure.

 The YELLOW LEVEL presents more challenging ideas, a broad vocabulary, and wide variety in sentence structure.

 The GREEN LEVEL presents more complex ideas, an extended vocabulary range, and expanded language structures.

 The ORANGE LEVEL presents a wide range of ideas and concepts using challenging vocabulary and complex language structures.

When sharing a content focused book with your child, read to find out facts and concepts, pausing often to restate and talk about the new information. The realistic story format provides an opportunity to talk about the language used, and to learn about reading to problem-solve for information. Encourage children to measure, make maps, and consider other situations that allow them to apply what they are learning.

There is no right or wrong way to share books with children. Find time to read and share new learning with your child, and pass on the legacy of literacy.

Adria F. Klein, Ph.D.
Professor Emeritus
California State University
San Bernardino, California

Editor: Shelly Lyons
Designer: Tracy Davies
Page Production: Ashlee Schultz
Art Director: Nathan Gassman
Associate Managing Editor: Christianne Jones
The illustrations in this book were created with soft pastels.

Picture Window Books
5115 Excelsior Boulevard
Suite 232
Minneapolis, MN 55416
877-845-8392
www.picturewindowbooks.com

Printed in the United States of America.

All books published by Picture Window Books
are manufactured with paper containing at least
10 percent post-consumer waste.

Library of Congress Cataloging-in-Publication Data
Gunderson, Jessica.
The moving carnival / by Jessica Gunderson ; illustrated by Caroline Jones McKay.
p. cm. — (Read-it! readers: science)
ISBN-13: 978-1-4048-4222-9 (library binding)
[1. Motion—Fiction.] I. McKay, Caroline Jones, ill. II. Title.
PZ7.G963Mov 2008
[E]—dc22   2007032905

THE MOVING CARNIVAL

by Jessica Gunderson
illustrated by Caroline Jones McKay

Special thanks to our advisers for their expertise:

Paul R. Ohmann, Ph.D.
Associate Professor of Physics
University of St. Thomas, St. Paul, Minnesota

Adria F. Klein, Ph.D.
Professor Emeritus, California State University
San Bernardino, California

PICTURE WINDOW BOOKS
Minneapolis, Minnesota

Luiz woke up early. He watched the hands on his clock move. His heart thumped. Today was going to be an exciting day.

Luiz waited until six o'clock. Then he jumped out of bed and ran to Rosa's room.

"Rosa," Luiz called to his sister. "Wake up!"

"It's too early," she groaned. Then she remembered that today was a special day.

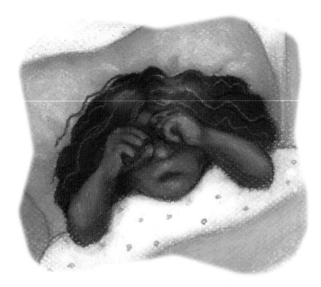

"We're going to the carnival!" she said, jumping out of bed.

Luiz and Rosa got dressed. Then they ran downstairs to eat breakfast.

After breakfast, Luiz and Rosa skipped and hopped along the sidewalk. They found a ball. Rosa kicked it high in the air.

Luiz caught the ball. He threw it back to Rosa. "There's no time to play," he said. "Let's hurry!"

Rosa stopped to tie
her shoe.

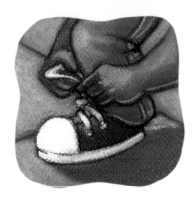

Then she stopped
to smell a tulip.

"Come on, Rosa," Luiz complained. "You are
too slow!"

"Let's run," Rosa said.

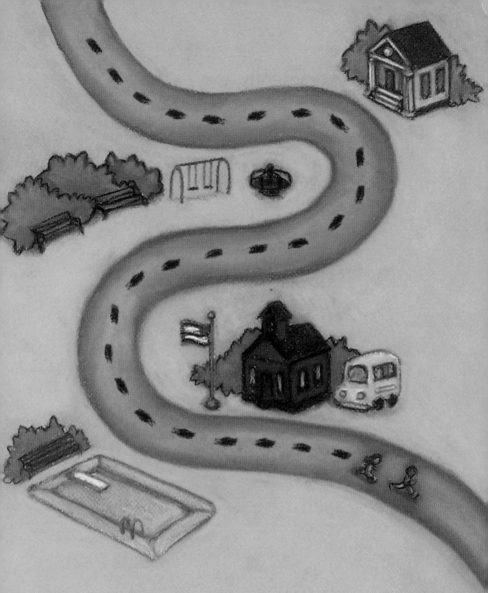

The children ran as fast as they could. They zoomed past the bank and the park. They raced past the school and the swimming pool. The wind whipped through their hair.

Luiz could not wait.
He wanted to float
toward the clouds on
the Ferris wheel.

He wanted to
zip through the
sky on the roller
coaster.

He wanted to spin in
the air on the Zipper.

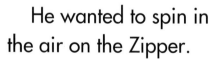

When Luiz and Rosa reached the carnival, they stopped in front of the Ferris wheel. Rosa looked up. She grabbed Luiz's arm. Her eyes grew large.

13

"Let's ride the Ferris wheel," Luiz said.

"Oh, no. Not me!" Rosa exclaimed.

Luiz knew Rosa was scared. "Let's ride the bumper cars first," he suggested.

"Sure," Rosa agreed. She loved bumping into the other cars.

You can move many objects by pushing or pulling. The more force you use to push an object, the farther and faster it will move. When one bumper car hits a second bumper car, the second car moves or spins. The faster the first car is moving when they hit, the greater the force it will have on the second car.

Luiz and Rosa got into their cars and buckled their seat belts. When the ride started, Rosa pushed the pedal. She steered her car toward Luiz's car. When the cars hit, Luiz's car spun around and around.

Rosa giggled. "I got you!" she said.

When an object is in motion, it stops only if some force stops it. When an object isn't moving, it stays still until a force moves it.

When Luiz's car stopped spinning, Luiz
asked, "Are you ready to ride the Ferris wheel?"
Rosa's lips trembled. "Oh, no. Not me!"
she said.

When they got off the bumper cars, Luiz and Rosa saw a clown sitting above a tank of water.

"Hit the target, and I'll fall into the water!" the clown shouted.

Rosa paid a dollar for three balls. She threw one ball at the target.

"You missed!" chuckled the clown.

Rosa squinted and aimed. She threw the second ball as hard as she could. The ball hit the center of the target. Splash! The clown fell into the water. Soon he rose to the surface.

Some objects float in water. Other objects sink. If an object weighs more than the weight of water it pushes away, the object will sink.

When Rosa finished playing the dunking game, Luiz asked, "Now are you ready for the Ferris wheel?"

"Oh, no. Not me!" she said.

"Then let's try the Tilt-a-Whirl," Luiz said.
Rosa nodded happily.

DUNK ME

On the Tilt-a-Whirl, the cars spun around and around. Luiz squeezed the metal bar. Rosa squeezed Luiz.

"Lean toward me," Luiz said. "Our car will spin in the direction we lean."

"OK," Rosa said. "But I can't look."
Rosa kept her eyes closed as they spun and whirled. When the ride slowed to a stop, she opened her eyes.
"That was fun!" she said.

Luiz and Rosa walked away from the Tilt-a-Whirl.

Luiz asked, "Now are you ready to ride the Ferris wheel?"

Rosa's eyes grew larger, but she nodded
and said, "Just once."

Up, up, up they went on the Ferris wheel.
Rosa kept her eyes closed. Luiz looked at
everything around him.

The people on the ground looked as small as ants. Luiz could see rooftops all across town. Then he saw a house that looked very familiar.

"Look, Rosa!" Luiz said.

Rosa opened one eye. Then she opened the other. "It's our house!" she exclaimed.

Luiz and Rosa looked around them as the world beneath them moved. Cars sped along the highway. An airplane flew across the sky. Even the clouds were moving.

Anything that goes from one place to another is in motion. Objects move forward and backward. They move in curved lines, straight lines, and zigzag lines. They also move at different speeds.

Luiz and Rosa smiled as they walked away from the Ferris wheel. "Next stop, the roller coaster," Luiz said.

"Oh, no. Not me!" Rosa said.

MOTION ACTIVITY

What you need:
- string
- a scissors
- two items of different weight (such as bolts)
- a hook or a rod
- a stopwatch
- a pen
- a notepad

What you do:
1. Cut one piece of string to a length of 3 feet (90 centimeters).
2. Tie the lighter weight to one end of the string.
3. Now tie a hook or rod to the other end of the string, and let the weight swing freely.
4. Push the weight lightly so it swings.
5. Time how long it takes for the weight to swing back and forth ten times, and write the time on the notepad.
6. Remove the weight from the string.
7. Repeat steps 2 through 6 with the heavier weight.
8. Next, cut another piece of string to a length of 2 feet (60 cm).
9. Repeat steps 2 through 6 with each of the weights.

Which weight took longer to swing back and forth ten times? Which string took longer to swing?

Glossary

force—any action that changes the movement of an object
motion—movement
speed—how fast an object moves from one place to another
weight—the measurement of how heavy an object or person is

To Learn More

More Books to Read

Gold-Dworkin, Heidi. *Learning About the Way Things Move.*
    New York: McGraw-Hill, 2001.
Morgan, Ben. *Motion.* San Diego: Blackbirch Press, 2003.
Stewart, Melissa. *Energy in Motion.* New York: Children's
    Press, 2006.
Stille, Darlene R. *Motion: Push and Pull, Fast and Slow.* Minneapolis:
    Picture Window Books, 2004.

On the Web

FactHound offers a safe, fun way to find Web sites related to
topics in this book. All of the sites on FactHound have been
researched by our staff.

1. Visit *www.facthound.com*
2. Type in this special code: 1404842225
3. Click on the FETCH IT button.

Your trusty FactHound will fetch the best sites for you!

Look for all of the books in the
Read-it! Readers: Science series:

Friends and Flowers (life science: bulbs)
The Grass Patch Project (life science: grass)
The Sunflower Farmer (life science: sunflowers)
Surprising Beans (life science: beans)

The Moving Carnival (physical science: motion)
A Secret Matter (physical science: matter)
A Stormy Surprise (physical science: electricity)
Up, Up in the Air (physical science: air)